Hooray for Mother's Day!

Based on the TV series *Little Bill*® created by Bill Cosby as seen on Nick Jr.®

ISBN 0-439-46294-0

Published by Scholastic Inc., 557 Broadway, New York, NY 10012, by arrangement with Simon Spotlight, Simon
& Schuster Children's Publishing Division. SCHOLASTIC and associated logos are trademarks
and/or registered trademarks of Scholastic Inc.

12 11 10 9 8 7 6 5 4 3 2 1   3 4 5 6 7 8/0

Printed in the U.S.A.
First Scholastic printing, April 2003

Hooray for Mother's Day!

by Catherine Lukas

illustrated by Bernie Cavender

SCHOLASTIC INC.

New York Toronto London Auckland Sydney
Mexico City New Delhi Hong Kong Buenos Aires

"Hooray! Hooray! It's Mother's Day!" sang Little Bill as he marched up to his mother, Brenda. His sister, April, and his brother, Bobby, followed close behind.

"Good morning, you all!" said Brenda.

"We brought you breakfast in bed," Bobby said.

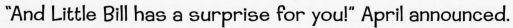

"And Little Bill has a surprise for you!" April announced.

"Not just one," said Little Bill. "I have *five* surprises, Mama, because I'm five."

"*Five* surprises?" asked Brenda. "Then I'd better hurry up and eat these delicious-looking pancakes. I can't wait to see what your surprises are!"

As soon as Brenda was dressed, Little Bill led her to the living room. "The first present is hidden in here," he said. "You can start looking, Mama. I'll tell you if you're getting close."

"Hmm," said Brenda, walking toward the sofa. "I wonder if it's over here—"

"You're warm!" said Little Bill.

She turned and headed toward Alice the Great.
"Uh-oh, you're getting colder," he said.
Brenda walked back over to the sofa.
"Oooh!" exclaimed Little Bill. "You're HOT! HOT! HOT!"
Brenda lifted up a cushion and looked underneath. "Well, look what I found!"

"What a beautiful wrapping job," said Brenda.
"I'll help you open it," said Little Bill eagerly. Together they tore away the paper.

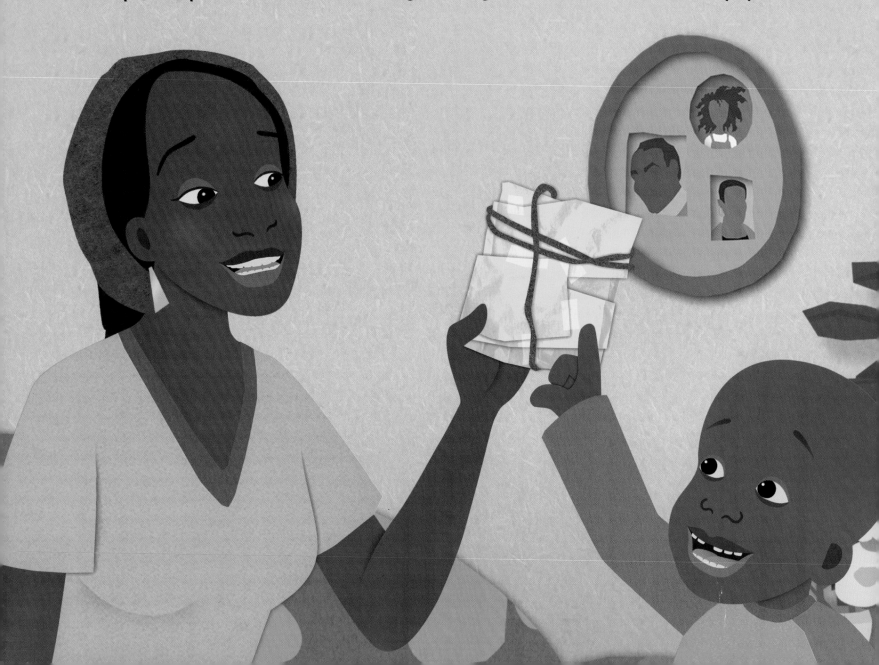

"Remember this picture you took, Mama?" asked Little Bill.

"Of course I do," said Brenda. "It's a picture of one of my favorite models. And look at this fabulous frame!"

"I decorated it all by myself," said Little Bill. "Now you have to find the second present. Come with me, Mama!"

They stepped out into the backyard. "Ready, Mama?" asked Little Bill.
"Your second present is here somewhere. I put it in something that's yellow."
   "Well, I see a few things that are yellow . . . ," said Brenda.
   Little Bill giggled. "This is a yellow thing you use to water the flowers."
   Brenda clapped her hands. "Then it must be the watering can!"
She peered into the watering can. "Ooh, I see something."

"Did you make this for me at school?" asked Brenda, admiring the gift.

"Yep. In art class," said Little Bill, beaming. "My teacher helped me."

"Is it supposed to lean to one side like that?" Bobby asked.

Little Bill's face fell, but Brenda hugged him tightly. "It's perfect for my hair clips, baby," she said. "I'll keep it on my dresser and think of you every time I look at it."

"For your third present," said Little Bill, reaching into his pocket, "you need to wear this." He pulled out a wrinkly bandanna.

"Is my hair that messy?" asked Brenda, laughing.

"No, Mama, it's a blindfold!" said Little Bill. "I'm taking you on an adventure to your next present!"

He led her through the kitchen, into the living room, and up the stairs.

"Now be careful and hold on tight, Mama," said Little Bill. "We're climbing a humongous mountain, and there's a big waterfall!"

"Sounds dangerous," said Brenda, clutching Little Bill's hand.

"Don't worry, Mama," he said. "I'll protect you. Ooh, watch out for the alligators. Just lift up your feet . . . almost there . . . we made it to the top!"

"Whew. That was close!" said Brenda.

They reached the door of Little Bill's room. "Are you ready, Mama?" he asked.

Brenda nodded. Little Bill opened the door, then pulled off the bandanna. "Ta-da!" he said.

Brenda looked around. "Little Bill!" she exclaimed. "What happened to your room? It's *spotless*."

"I cleaned it all by myself," said Little Bill happily. "I even straightened up Elephant's cage!"

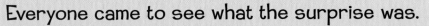

Everyone came to see what the surprise was.

"Pretty good job, Little Bill," said Bobby.

Big Bill chuckled. "I hope Father's Day is this exciting!"

"Okay, Mama," said Little Bill eagerly, "for your fourth present you have to come down to the kitchen."

"Is the kitchen spotless too?"
Brenda asked, laughing.

Bobby, April, and Big Bill followed Little Bill and Brenda into the kitchen. "Sit right here, Mama," said Little Bill, pulling out a chair.

Brenda sat down at the table.

Little Bill pulled out a large, folded piece of paper. "For your fourth present, Mama, I made you a menu. You can have *anything* you want."

Brenda studied the menu. "The peanut-butter-and-jelly sandwich looks good," she said. "May I have that, with a glass of milk, please?"

"Sure!" said Little Bill. "You want Dad to cut off the crusts for you?"

Brenda looked over at Big Bill. "I'll have it however the chef wants to make it."

Little Bill and Big Bill got busy. A few moments later Little Bill brought the sandwich and glass of milk to his mother. "Here you go, Mama," he said proudly.

"Little Bill," said Bobby, "Mama just ate breakfast. It's not time for lunch."

"Shh, Bobby," April said, "it's Little Bill's present."

Little Bill looked worriedly at Brenda. "Are you hungry, Mama?" he asked.

"I'm *starved*," said Brenda, picking up the sandwich. "My breakfast in bed feels like it was ages ago." She took a big bite. "Mmm, this is the most delicious sandwich I have ever eaten. In fact," she said, putting it down on the plate, "it's so good, I don't want to eat it all at once. I'm going to save it for later."

Little Bill giggled. "That's okay, Mama. You can take your time to eat it, 'cause Mother's Day is *all* day."

"And now it's time for the last present," said Little Bill, as Alice the Great came into the kitchen. Winking at Little Bill, she handed him one end of a piece of yarn.

Little Bill turned to Brenda. "Here, Mama," he said, giving her the end of the yarn. "Follow this yarn and you'll find your fifth present!"

Brenda followed the yarn trail from the kitchen . . .
through the living room . . .

up the stairs . . .

down the hall . . .

and into Little Bill's bedroom.

"Where is the yarn taking me?" Brenda asked as she followed the yarn trail. "What's at the other end? A kite? A sweater?" The yarn led her over by Elephant's cage, then around Little Bill's bed.

"No, nothing back here," she said, still following the yarn. "Aha. It's leading me to the closet," she said. Brenda slowly opened the door and peered inside. "It's . . . it's . . ."

"It's ME!" yelled Little Bill, jumping up. "Your last present is a big hug from me! Happy Mother's Day, Mama!"

"And it's the best present of all," said Brenda. "Thank you for a wonderful Mother's Day, Little Bill."